LOST!

BODEGA

by Maria Bates
illustrated by C. Shana Greger

ISBN 0-15-317246-0 – Lost!

Ordering Options
ISBN 0-15-318629-1 (Package of 5)
ISBN 0-15-316986-9 (Grade 2 Package)

3 4 5 6 7 8 9 10 179 02 01 00

The little cat, Pepe, was very unhappy.
He had sneaked into the car so he could go
with the girl. At the market he had run
after some mice. Now he was lost.

1

Pepe looked everywhere for the girl.
He ran up and down and here and there.
He couldn't find the girl anywhere.
Where was he? Was he thousands of
miles from home?

"I'm not really thousands of miles
from home," he thought. "I'll find my
way home."

Pepe walked through the large market. He saw many fruits and vegetables and meats. Pepe was hungry. He was happy when a man gave him scraps of meat and fish. They tasted good to a hungry cat!

3

At the end of the market, Pepe saw an
exhibition of dancing. Ladies in bright
dresses were turning around and around.
The exhibition was fun to watch. There
were many people watching and taking
photographs. Pepe had to be careful so he
wouldn't be stepped on!

The girl's family was in the landscape
business. So Pepe knew about landscape.
The landscape near the market was very
flat. The landscape near his home was hilly.
So Pepe set off toward the hills.

5

After a while, Pepe came to a ranch.
There were a lot of brown horses on the
ranch. There were a few dappled horses,
too. Pepe stopped to lap up some milk
from a pail near the barn. The dappled
horses seemed to laugh at him. Pepe just
groomed himself and went on.

Soon Pepe came to a town. People
were everywhere, playing music and
singing. There were a lot of dogs, too.
This was not a good place for a cat!
So Pepe went on.

Pepe walked by a place to eat. A kind
lady gave him some water and some scraps
of food. He felt much stronger after a good
meal. Now Pepe didn't feel so unhappy. He
felt as if he would make it home.

8

Pepe came to another town. He saw
the street signs. He wished he could read
so he would know where he was. Then,
when Pepe turned the corner, he saw a
cat he knew. "I must be almost home!"
he thought.

Pepe began sniffing the ground and the air. He would sniff his way home! Finally he saw the family's landscape business. There was the girl! She was playing in the yard.

The girl looked up and saw Pepe.
"Where have you been? I've been
looking for you everywhere. I'm so glad
you're back!"

The girl gave the little cat an enormous
hug. Then she rubbed his chin just the way
he liked.

The girl brushed Pepe's dirty coat.
Soon he was clean again. Pepe had been
brave and smart and strong. He had
made it home!

Pepe's Path

Show what happened in *Lost!*. Copy each sentence and blank below on a sheet of paper. Write 1, 2, 3, 4, 5, and 6 to put the sentences in story order. (Turn the page to find the answers.)

_____ Pepe sees a cat he knows.

_____ A man at the market gives Pepe scraps of meat and fish.

_____ Pepe walks to a ranch.

_____ Pepe finds the girl and his home.

_____ At the market, Pepe runs after some mice and gets lost.

_____ Pepe watches an exhibition of dancing.

 School-Home Connection Invite your child to read *Lost!* to you. Ask whether your child thinks Pepe will sneak away again.

Just in Time
Use with "Anthony Reynoso: Born to Rope."

Answers:

5	Pepe sees a cat he knows.
2	A man at the market gives Pepe scraps of meat and fish.
4	Pepe walks to a ranch.
6	Pepe finds the girl and his home.
1	At the market, Pepe runs after some mice and gets lost.
3	Pepe watches an exhibition of dancing.